Broccoli-Flavored Bubble Gum

Story by Justin McGivern

Illustrations by Patrick Girouard

RSVP

RAINTREE STECK-VAUGHN
PUBLISHERS

The Steck-Vaughn Company

Austin, Texas

To my wonderful family,
especially my loving and caring mom and dad;
to my grandparents for all their love and support;
to Dr. Gerald E. Porter and the rest of the staff at the Marshfield Clinic;
and to all my cool friends and fun teachers. — J.M.

For Marc and Max, who always eat their vegetables,
and Rita, who seldom does. — P.G.

Library of Congress Cataloging-in-Publication Data

McGivern, Justin, 1985 –
    Broccoli-flavored bubble gum / story by Justin McGivern ; illustrations by Patrick Girouard.
        p.   cm. — (Publish-a-book)
    Summary: A young boy's inventions of new food combinations, such as broccoli-flavored bubble gum, cauliflower cookies, and carrot candy, bring him fame and fortune.
    ISBN 0–8172–4425–5
    1. Children's writings, American.   [1. Inventions — Fiction.   2. Food — Fiction.   3. Children's writings.]
I. Girouard, Patrick, ill.   II. Title.   III. Series.
PZ7.M478475Br   1996
[E] — dc20   95-25691
        3-14-96   CIP   AC

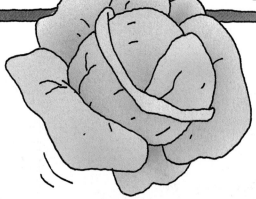

"The future of the nation looks bleak. The kids are not eating their vegetables. Without the vitamins and nutrients in vegetables, our future adults will be tiny, wimpy, and not very intelligent."

That was the message the President gave the country over national television.

I was chewing some bubble gum, sitting on the couch, watching TV, trying to think of something to do for the science fair. My mother called me to the supper table.

I forgot to spit my gum out before starting to eat supper, so I stuck it between my teeth and my cheek. When we got toward the end of supper, I was talking to my parents when I accidentally started chewing on some broccoli, which is something I rarely do. One thing led to another and before I knew it, I was chewing on broccoli-flavored bubble gum! And you know what? It tasted good! In fact, it tasted GREAT! That's when the idea hit me — broccoli-flavored bubble gum — what a way to eat vegetables! This could solve our nation's problem! I could become famous. I could become a millionaire!

Right away my mind started thinking of all the other combinations I could make, like cauliflower cookies, spinach soda pop, carrot candy, cucumber cake, and lima bean brownies. I had found my idea for the science fair!

Science Fair
FREE
SAMPLES

8

At the science fair I gave out free samples of my new vegetable-flavored favorite foods. I didn't let anybody know what was in them. Everybody loved them! The kids and the judges said things like, "I've never tasted anything so good!" and "What is this made of? These are excellent!" All my samples were gone in the first fifteen minutes of the science fair, and I won first prize.

I got to take my science project to the state competition. I won there, too! Finally, I got to go to the national competition, which was in Washington, D.C. The grand prize was a chance to meet the President and have my invention put on the market.

As luck would have it, I won the grand prize at the national competition, too. Later that day, I met the President. She tried some of my samples. She especially liked the pickle pizza. She told me I was a genius, and that my invention would save the country.

I became independently wealthy. My food inventions were sold everywhere. They were advertised on TV during the Saturday morning cartoons. I got more money than I could even count! I was famous!

The nation's kids were demanding more and more new flavors. I invented green pepper popcorn, red rutabaga licorice, black Brussels sprout licorice, turnip taffy, and mushroom milk shakes. Water chestnut chocolate wafers were an absolute favorite.

Zany zucchini and sauerkraut sherbet was soon sold out of all the local grocery stores. The kids really loved my invention of cabbage cake. Even babies were more content with my French onion formula!

Candy stores everywhere
stocked my new line of vegetables.
Fast-food restaurants featured them.

I was soon asked to create specialty items like pea pod pasta for professional sports players who used them right before big games. This delicious food combination gave them extra energy to score and win. They even set new records.

I created an artichoke and asparagus drink that was combined with either regular or diet soda pop for astronauts. It was easy to drink and could keep them awake for longer time periods.

I was a busy inventor and received many awards. But probably the most important one to me was the Nobel Prize.

One night after things had settled down a bit, I was watching TV and chewing on broccoli-flavored bubble gum when a special news bulletin came on from the President.

She said, "Now we have a new problem facing our country. Our nation's adults are not eating their vegetables. Without the vitamins and nutrients in vegetables, adults will be weak, crabby, and tired all the time."

I quickly turned off the TV. "Back to the drawing board," I said. "Hmmm…how about tangy tomato-flavored tea, kohlrabi coffee, or mocha-flavored mashed eggplant?" This was going to be a bit more of a challenge!

Justin McGivern, the author of **Broccoli-Flavored Bubble Gum**, was born on February 6, 1985, in Wausau, Wisconsin. He is the fifth generation to live in the Wausau area. His mother and father both have careers in the art field. His dad, Andrew, is Curator of Exhibitions at the Leigh Yawkey Woodson Art Museum in Wausau, and his mom, Jeana, is an art teacher for the Wausau School District. Both parents are artists as well, so Justin has been "brainwashed" to believe that art is one of the most important things in life! Justin is a good artist himself. He has won numerous drawing and art contests. His favorite was a contest in which he was asked to donate his prize money to a charity. He chose UNICEF because he liked the idea of kids helping other kids.

Justin also enjoys sports. He fell in love with soccer at age five and continues this passion to the present. He plays "striker" on his team and loves to make goals! Justin's other sports passion is basketball. He plays daily and is coached and encouraged by his Uncle Darrel during their weekend "tournaments."

Justin's love for sports keeps him very fit and healthy, which is fortunate because in August of 1993 Justin was diagnosed with Type I diabetes. Justin keeps tight control of his blood sugars through diet,

insulin therapy, and exercise. He does not let diabetes run his life; however, controlling diabetes is the main reason he knows so much about food!

Justin is fortunate to have a caring extended family. In his toddler years, when both his parents were working, he was given the best of care by his Grandma Esther and Grandpa Fred Jaeger, from whom he picked up his great sense of humor. His Grandma Joan and his uncles and aunts have given him tremendous support and encouragement, too.

Likewise, Justin has had great teachers at his school, Lincoln Elementary, where he is currently in the Gifted and Talented Magnet Program. He has had to write a lot for his teacher, Mrs. Barbara Klofstad, who is his sponsor in the 1995 Publish-a-Book™ Contest. He has learned to use his flair for humor in his writings. Justin attributes his love for books and reading to the countless number of books read to him by his family, and to his frequent visits to the Marathon County Public Library.

The twenty honorable-mention winners in the **1995 Raintree/Steck-Vaughn Publish-a-Book™ Contest** were Mike Asmar, Boulan Park Middle School, Troy, Michigan; Catie Myers-Wood, Grey Culbreth Middle School, Chapel Hill, North Carolina; Stephanie Iannucci, St. Callistus School, Philadelphia, Pennsylvania; Mavis Morse, Hermon Elementary School, Bangor, Maine; Tina Addington, Rorimer Elementary School, LaPuente, California; Fred Barr, Cape Christian Academy, Cape May, New Jersey; Benjamin J. Brotsker, E. A. Tighe School, Margate, New Jersey; Katherine E. Coons, Haycock Elementary School, Falls Church, Virginia; Marwin Hunte, P.S. 203, Brooklyn, New York; Gary Kenneth Burrell, Jr., Sinclair Lane Elementary School, Baltimore, Maryland; Mary Elizabeth Smith, St. Rose of Lima School, Haddon Heights, New Jersey; Jonathan P. Walsh, Haycock Elementary School, Falls Church, Virginia; Daniel Ross Walt, Quincy Public Library, Quincy, Illinois; Brynn Cahill, Central Middle School, San Carlos, California; Emmy Ogle, Sierra Oaks School, Sacramento, California; Nicholas A. Langston, Iuka Elementary School, Iuka, Mississippi; Kate Zimmermann, M. H. Burnett Elementary School, Wilmington, Delaware; Allison Condon, Peter Noyes School, Sudbury, Massachusetts; Ryan Dixon, Riverside Elementary School, Moorhead, Minnesota; Julie Young, St. Ann's Academy, Calhoun, Georgia.

Patrick Girouard loves to make pictures. He is frequently advised on color and content by his sons, Marc and Max. Patrick's favorite vegetables include onions, mushrooms, broccoli, and spinach; he dislikes Brussels sprouts and squash. He says he can converse with dogs, hold his breath for a very long time, and has the strength of ten men.